PTERANODON

THE LIFE STORY OF A PTEROSAUR

by RUTH ASHBY

illustrations by PHIL WILSON

HARRY N. ABRAMS, INC., PUBLISHERS

The place is North America. The time is long, long ago. Dinosaurs roam the earth and flying reptiles cruise the skies. On a cliff high above the warm, wide Niobrara Sea, a brown speckled egg sits in the sun.

Tap! Tap! Tap! comes a noise from inside. First a sharp little bill pokes out. Then a fuzzy head emerges. Dripping wet, a chick pushes out of the shell.

A baby *Pteranodon* has hatched! Worn out, he
rests beneath his mother, who keeps him warm.

A long shadow falls over the nest. The young *Pteranodon*'s father is back from a fishing trip, with food for his hatchling. Excited, the chick begins to peck at his father's long bill.

He is hungry!

Father opens his beak, and the chick gulps down his first meal of fish. Until he can fly, his mother and father will take turns feeding him. Then he will be on his own.

After a few weeks, the chick begins to explore his world. Crawling on all fours, he ventures away from the nest. Sometimes he loses his balance and tips over, but he always scrambles up and tries again.

Soon he practices spreading his leathery wings and facing into the wind. One day he finds himself up in the air, and — **whoosh!** — he is flying. Startled, he quickly folds his wings and drops back to the ledge again. Then he tries once more. Within a few weeks, he is flying like a pro.

After a few months, *Pteranodon* is almost half-grown and ready to leave his cliffside home. He spreads his wings wide, a gust of warm air lifts him up, and off he soars, high over the waves.

And what a view! Sea and forest, beach and distant
mountains spread before him. On the shore below is a herd
of migrating hadrosaurs.

Pteranodon spies a school of *Enchodus* fish. He folds back his ten-foot-long wings and dives. Nearing the surface of the water, he aims for a fish, then reaches down with his razor-sharp beak. **SNATCH!**

He has it! He turns and climbs to dive again and again, catching some fish, losing others. Before long, his stomach is full. *Pteranodon* has had a successful first hunt.

There are many dangers to avoid in the Niobrara Sea.
Every day *Pteranodon* must risk his life for food. The trick is
to find a meal without becoming one!

One day he joins a group of *Ichthyornids*, early sea birds, feasting on a school of fish. Just as he swoops down to scoop up a fish, a bird darts in and steals it. Frustrated, *Pteranodon* dives again. He does not notice a dark head rising from the water . . .

... a deadly ELASMOSAURUS is on the prowl!

The giant reptile rears its twenty-foot-long neck—and strikes. It seizes one *Ichthyornid* in its spike-toothed mouth, devouring it instantly. The flying creatures scatter.

Pteranodon, too, tries to fly out of harm's way. But *Elasmosaurus* crashes into him—and *Pteranodon* tumbles into the water.

Meanwhile, a second savage hunter arrives to join the party!

Tylosaurus, another marine reptile, glides in and gulps down another bird. Angered, *Elasmosaurus* turns on the beast and bites a chunk out of its scaly hide. *Tylosaurus* opens its huge jaws and charges.

Pteranodon struggles in the water. Is he injured? Carefully, he spreads his wings to check. No broken bones! A warm breeze lifts him into the air, and he escapes. As he flies off, the bloody battle continues to rage below. *Pteranodon* is lucky to be alive!

As the months slip by, *Pteranodon* grows and learns. One morning, he starts up from his sandy bed and spreads his wings. He senses danger. Before he can rise into the air, a raptor suddenly darts out from the underbrush. It leaps and slashes *Pteranodon*'s wing. Startled, *Pteranodon* jabs at his enemy with his beak.

Another raptor has shown up to join the attack. Now, four large, shining eyes fasten on young *Pteranodon* as the raptors circle their prey. Suddenly, the ground shakes.

SOMETHING ELSE IS COMING!

A huge head pokes out of the trees—

TYRANNOSAURUS REX!

Roaring, the giant predator comes up behind one of the raptors. It snatches up the smaller dinosaur in its powerful jaws.

Pteranodon is now desperate. He must escape
or be eaten! With two great flaps of his
wings, he is in the air and out of danger.

He barely notices the tear in his leathery wing.
The wound will heal.

Pteranodon is safe. But he has learned his lesson.
He will try to sleep on the cliffs from now on.

Five years pass. Now *Pteranodon* is a full-grown adult, with a wingspan of twenty-eight feet. His bright crest soars three feet above his head. His swordlike bill is almost as long.

Late one winter, he feels an urge, an instinct he cannot resist. Something inside tells him he must return home. He sets off on a journey across the sea. Soon, he is joined by others. The air is thick with male pterosaurs in flight.

Pteranodon lands on the cliff where he was born. He must find a place for a nest. Looking around, he spies an unclaimed spot and moves toward a sandy mound surrounded by ferns. But another male swaggers up to the mound, flashing his colorful crest and pointing his bill to the sky.

Pteranodon takes the challenge. He lashes out at the intruder with his bill. Back and forth they fight.

WHACK! WHACK! WHACK!

Pteranodon delivers a final, loud blow. The other male stumbles and backs away. Victory! *Pteranodon* has won his mound.

Early one morning, *Pteranodon* looks up to see dozens
of wings darkening the sky.

The females have arrived!

All day long they parade in front of the males. *Pteranodon* struts and stretches, showing off his handsome head crest. One female stops and shakes her head at him. He shakes his crest back. He calls. She answers. They begin their mating dance. By evening, the female has made her decision. She settles herself in the middle of *Pteranodon's* mound. This is where she will make her nest.

A week later, *Pteranodon* and his mate are the parents of a speckled egg. They take turns keeping it warm. In a month, another funny-looking hatchling will be born. *Pteranodon* will be a father, and the cycle of life will be complete.

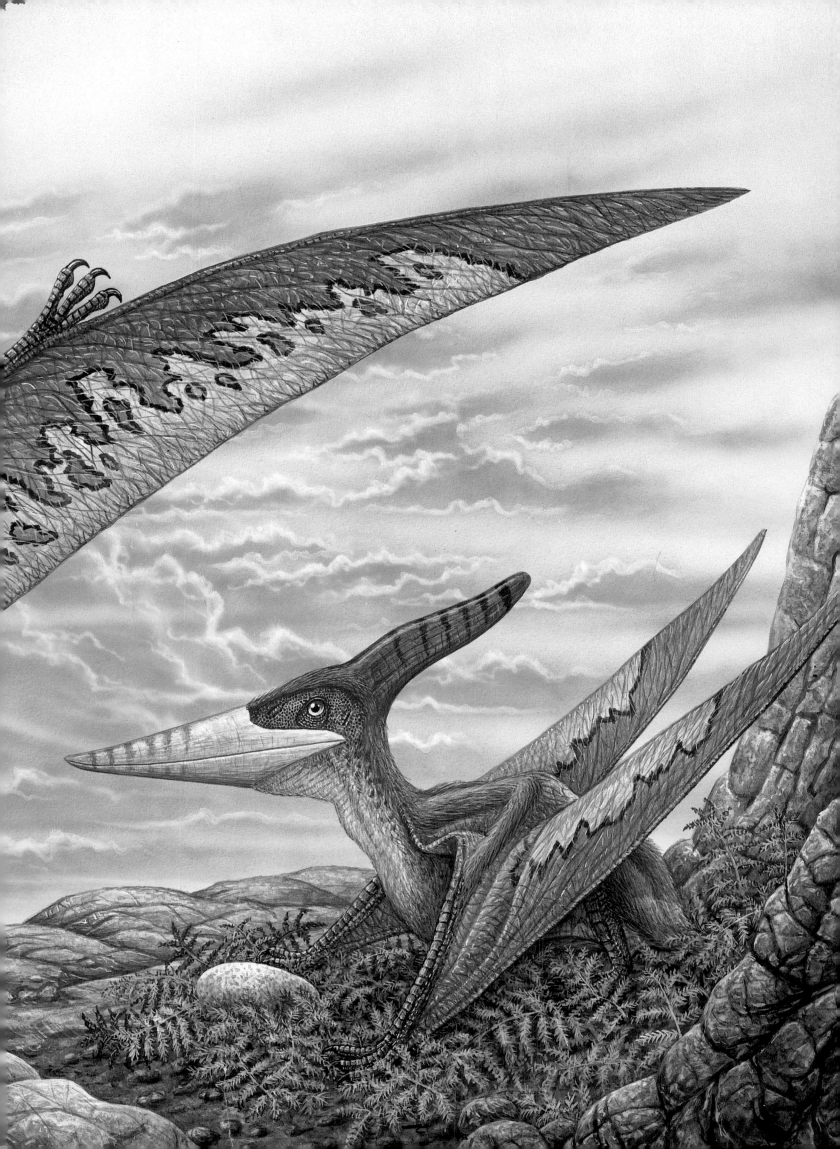

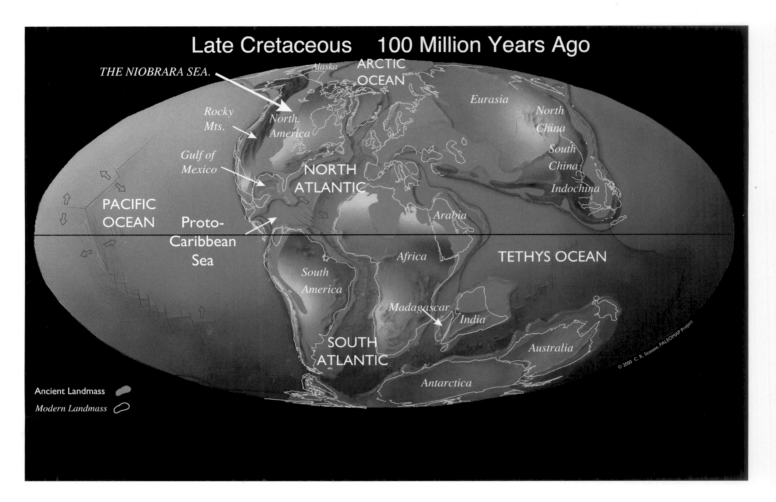

The Cretaceous Period lasted from 146 million years ago until 65 million years ago. This map shows how the landmasses of the planet looked at the time of our story, 100 million years ago. The white outlines denote the modern shapes of the continents as we know them today.

Our story takes place on the shores of the shallow inland sea of North America that existed during the Cretaceous, called the Niobrara. Today's Great Plains of the western United States are actually the floor of this ancient inland sea.

GLOSSARY

Cretaceous (kree-TAY-shus): the geologic period of time between 146 and 65 million years ago. The third and final period of the Mesozoic Era.

Dinosaurs (DIE-no-sawrs): A successful and varied group of land animals with fully upright postures that lived throughout the Mesozoic Era. Until recently, crocodilians (such as crocodiles and similar reptiles) have been thought of as the dinosaurs' closest living relatives. However, there is now much evidence to suggest that dinosaurs were closer to birds than reptiles, and that birds may have actually evolved from small, meat-eating, warm-blooded dinosaurs.

Enchodus (en-KO-duss): fanged fish that lived during the Cretaceous period.

Elasmosaurus (ee-laz-muh-SAW-rus): a long-necked plesiosaur (marine reptile) that lived in the seas of North America and eastern Asia during the Late Cretaceous period.

Hadrosaurs (HAD-ro-sawrs): a group of plant-eating dinosaurs often referred to as "duck bills." Hadrosaur means "bulky reptile."

Hatchling: a newly hatched animal.

Ichthyornids (ick-thee-OR-nids): toothed birds that lived in North America during the Mid- to Late Cretaceous period.

Mesozoic (mez-o-ZOE-ik): the period of time from 245 million years ago up until 65 million years ago, when dinosaurs lived. This period is also referred to as the Age of Dinosaurs.

Niobrara Sea (nee-oh-BRAH-rah SEE): shallow interior sea that once covered the Great Plains of the North American continent. It stretched from what's now the Gulf of Mexico up into Canada.

Plesiosaurs (PLEZ-ee-uh-sawrs): marine reptiles with stout bodies, long necks, short tails, and four flippers. They lived in seas and oceans during the Mesozoic Era.

Pteranodon (TERR-an-UH-don): large flying reptile that lived in North America in the Mid- and Late Cretaceous periods.

Pterosaurs (TERR-uh-sawrs): general name for all of the flying reptiles of the Mesozoic Era.

Raptors (RAP-tores): small-to-midsize two-legged, meat-eating dinosaurs. Many species had a scythe-like retractable claw on each foot.

Reptiles (REP-tie-uhls): a class of air-breathing, cold-blooded vertebrates that includes alligators, crocodiles, lizards, snakes, turtles, and their extinct relatives.

Tylosaurus (tie-luh-SAW-rus): marine reptile with large head, long tail and short neck that lived in North American and New Zealand waters during the Late Cretaceous period.

Tyrannosaurus rex (tie-RAN-uh-SAW-rus REKS): largest two-legged, meat-eating dinosaur that lived in western North America during the Late Cretaceous period.

SELECT BIBLIOGRAPHY

Carpenter, Kenneth. *Eggs, Nests, and Baby Dinosaurs.* Bloomington: Indiana University Press, 1999.

Colagrande, John, and Larry Felder. *In the Presence of Dinosaurs.* Alexandria, VA: Time-Life Books, 2000.

Ellis, Richard. "Terrible Lizards of the Sea: When Dinosaurs Ruled the Land, Other Giant Reptiles Stalked the Deep." *Natural History*, (September 2003).

Fisher, Mildred L. *The Albatross of Midway Island: A Natural History of the Laysan Albatross.* Carbondale, IL: Southern Illinois University Press, 1970.

McGowan, Christopher. *Dinosaurs, Spitfires, and Sea Dragons.* Cambridge, MA: Harvard University Press, 1991.

Monasterky, Richard. "Pterosaurs: Lords of the Ancient Skies." *National Geographic* (May 2001).

Scotese, C. R. *Atlas of Earth History*, Volume I, Paleogeography, PALEOMAP Project, Arlington, Texas, 2001.

Wellnhofer, Peter. *The Illustrated Encyclopedia of Prehistoric Flying Reptiles.* New York: Barnes and Noble Books, 1991.

Zimmer, Carl. "Masters of an Ancient Sky." *Discover*, (February 1997).

Web Sites:

www.enchantedlearning.com/subjects/dinosaurs.html

www.oceansofkansas.com

www.ucmp.berkeley.edu/diapsids/pterosauria.html

ladywildlife.com/leopardsealspages/Pteranodon.html

AUTHOR'S NOTE

As both an editor and a writer, I have worked on books about dinosaurs and their prehistoric relatives for almost twenty years. Relating the life story of a *Pteranodon* was a special challenge because there is a lot we still don't know about these fascinating flyers. Most scientists agree, though, that pterosaurs were probably a lot like birds in their ability to fly, as well as their social structure and child-rearing techniques. Noted paleontologist Robert Bakker points out that pterosaur wings were supported by powerful breast and arm muscles, indicating exceptional flying ability. Like ocean-going birds such as the albatross, *Pteranodon* would have soared over great distances, kept aloft on warm air currents, or thermals. Bakker, Peter Wellnhofer, Chistopher MacGowen and others also reason that the pelvis of female pterosaurs was too narrow to allow for live births unless the newborns were indeed very tiny and immature. Most likely, pterosaurs, like birds, laid eggs. The helpless young would have remained in nests after hatching to be raised and fed by one or both parents. Field studies of the albatross help us envision *Pteranodon* mating displays and mating dances.

ARTIST'S NOTE

To envision how the creatures of the prehistoric past must have looked, I use a combination of photos of actual fossils and drawings made of skeletal reconstructions. I like to stay current with the latest findings as reported in various scientific journals such as *Scientific American*, *National Geographic* and *Nature*, and I enjoy occasional trips to Pittsburgh's own Carnegie Museum, which houses a world-famous dinosaur collection. There, with my sketchbook and camera in hand, I gather reference material for future paintings.

I have worked closely with renowned paleontologists Jack Horner and Peter Dobson on various publications concerning prehistoric life, and have valued their expertise immensely in interpreting the look and habitats of these animals.

Colorations, of course, are up to interpretation. Just as many birds' plumage displays today are brightly patterned to attract mates and to allow easy recognition for others of their kind, I believe that the pterosaur's crests played a similar role. Recent fossil finds have shown beyond a doubt that pterosaurs had a body covering of fine "fur" or downlike feathers, so I have included that feature in my illustrations. Scientists also believe that these creatures lived on or around high cliffs near bodies of water in order to take advantage of thermal air currents to aid them in their take-off and flight. Hence the settings chosen for this book.

Design: Gilda Hannah
Production Manager: Jonathan Lopes
Text copyright © 2005 Ruth Ashby
Illustrations copyright © 2005 Phil Wilson

Library of Congress Cataloging-in-Publication Data

Ashby, Ruth.
Pteranodon : the life story of a pterosaur / by Ruth Ashby ; art by Phil Wilson.
p. cm.
ISBN 0-8109-5778-7
1. Pteranodon—Juvenile literature. I. Wilson, Phil, ill. II. Title.

QE862.P7A84 2005
567.918—dc22
2004015612

Printed and bound in China
10 9 8 7 6 5 4 3 2 1

Harry N. Abrams, Inc.
100 Fifth Avenue
New York, NY 10011
www.abramsbooks.com

Abrams is a subsidiary of

LA MARTINIÈRE
GROUPE